Nicki Weiss

A Family Story

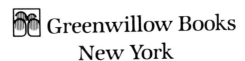 Greenwillow Books
New York

Gouache paints and colored pencils were used for the full-color art. The typeface is ITC Zapf International.

Copyright © 1987 by Monica J. Weiss All rights reserved. No part of this book may be reproduced without permission in writing from Greenwillow Books, 105 Madison Ave., N.Y. 10016.

Printed in Hong Kong by South China Printing Co.

First Edition
10 9 8 7 6 5 4 3 2 1

Library of Congress Cataloging-in-Publication Data
Weiss, Nicki. A family story.
Summary: Younger sister admires older sister, whose daughter admires aunt, and so it continues down the family line for generations.
[1. Sisters—Fiction. 2. Aunts—Fiction. 3. Cousins—Fiction] I. Title. PZ7.W448145Fam 1986 [E]
85-27231 ISBN 0-688-06504-X
ISBN 0-688-06505-8 (lib. bdg.)

For Walter and Ruth, Peter and Jenny, and Lilly

The day her sister Annie was born, Rachel was there.

In time, Rachel helped Annie into the stroller,
and Annie let no one but Rachel push.

When Rachel put on a shawl
and pretended to be Mama,
Annie put on a scarf and
pretended to be Rachel.

Rachel went to summer camp, and Annie
sent her paintings she had made at home.

Rachel grew out of her pink dress,
and Annie hung it in her closet
for when she would fit into it.

Annie went to summer camp, and Rachel
was her arts-and-crafts counselor.

Rachel got married, and Annie walked
down the aisle throwing flowers,
wearing the pink dress.

The day Rachel's daughter Louise was born,
Annie was there.

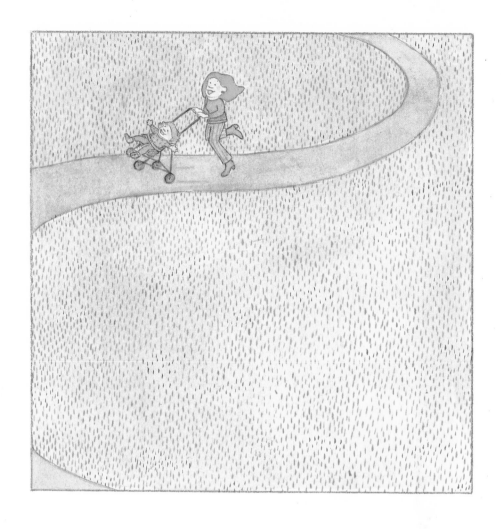

In time, Aunt Annie helped Louise into
the stroller and yelled, "Wheelies!" as
the two of them spun around.

Aunt Annie dressed up as Louise for
Halloween, and Louise dressed up
as Aunt Annie.

Aunt Annie took a trip to Mexico
and sent Louise postcards signed,
"I love you, Aunt Annie."

Louise went to summer camp and
sent Aunt Annie letters signed,
"I love you, Louise."

Aunt Annie cut her long hair short, and
Louise saved the ribbons for when her hair
would be long enough to wear them.

Aunt Annie got married, and Louise was
the flower girl, with ribbons in her hair.

The day Aunt Annie's daughter Jane
was born, Louise was there.

"No, no, no!" Jane shouted when anyone but Louise tried to push the stroller.

"My name is Annie," Louise said
when they played pretend.
"My name is Louise," said Jane.

And so on.

And so on.